D1597197

Papa Joe's Boys

Papa Joe's Boys

The Jacksons Story

Leonard Pitts, Jr.

STARBOOKS
SHARON PUBLICATIONS INC.
Cresskill, N.J.

This is a Star Book.

Copyright © 1983 by Sharon Publications, Inc. Photos used in this volume supplied by *Right On!* Magazine. All rights reserved. No part of this work may be reproduced or transmitted in any form or by any means, electronic or mechanical, including photocopying and recording, or by any information storage or retrieval system without permission in writing from the publisher.

All correspondence and inquiries should be directed to Sales Dept., Sharon Publications, Inc., 105 Union Avenue, Cresskill, New Jersey 07626.

Second Printing January 1984

Third Printing February 1984

Fourth Printing March 1984

Editor: Mary J. Edrei
Cover design by:
Mike Stromberg
Designed by Rod Gonzalez

Manufactured in the United States of America.

Sharon Publications is an Edrei Communications Company

ISBN # 0-89531-037-6

CONTENTS

Very Special People

My first impression of the Jacksons, whom I originally met in 1976, was that they were, indeed, a set of very, very special people, brought into this world by very special parents. All of them possess qualities of determination, perseverance and raw talent which has set them head and shoulders above any entertainers who have ever entered the business.

There will never be another set of entertainers who reach the level of success of the Jacksons. Not in the same way, at least and probably not in our lifetime. They are a caliber of people who were molded in a unique way. This mold was then broken.

They deserve it all: The constant adulation from fans during their concert appearances, the consistent sales of records which now stands at well over one hundred million and the admiration and respect from the entire industry.

Yes, Papa Joe's sons have done him proud!

Cynthia Horner
Editor
Right On! Magazine

THE JACKSON FIVE AND JOHNNY

Born To Entertain

J oe Jackson had it in his blood. That's how it really started. His dream was to be a star musician. There's a funny thing about dreams, though. They demand energy. They require that the dreamer hold them tight and guard them jealously, lest they melt away in the cold, bright light of reality.

Perhaps that's what happened to Jackson. Jackson, with wife Katherine, settled into a modest home in the industrial town of Gary, Indiana and before you could say "morning sickness," he had a house full of babies to support. Maureen came first. She was followed, in short order, by Sigmund, Toriano, Jermaine, LaToya, Marlon, Michael, Steven and Janet.

Papa Joe Jackson didn't need to have a house fall on him. He had been singing and playing lead guitar with the Falcons, a five-man act that played bars and colleges, but never managed any real success. But, with the babies coming and his household

expanding so fast, Jackson knew it was time to defer his life's dream; he put that dream and his guitar on the same shelf and concentrated on being a family man.

Another funny thing about dreams. For all their frailty and unpredictability, they die hard. Maybe that's the reason Jackson, working as a crane operator in one of Gary's countless factories, kept that old guitar around—as a sentimental reminder of an old dream. That also goes a long way toward explaining his reaction the day one of the kids—young Toriano—snuck the guitar out to fool around with it and broke a string in the process. Jackson, a stern, authoritarian father who was more than a little generous with the rod, wasn't exactly thrilled by this violation of his prized possession.

In an interview with *Crawdaddy*, Michael recalled the incident. "My father got mad," he said, "so *angry* and he said, 'Tito, sit down. I wanna see if you can play that guitar. If you can't, I'm really gonna *beat* you.'"

9

Joseph Jackson, father of the legendary Jacksons, recognized the talents of his sons early in life at the urging of his wife Katherine. Below: Katherine said in the early days, the family rehearsed and performed as a method of alleviating boredom.

Luckily, this wasn't the first time Toriano Adaryll "Tito" Jackson had ventured into the master bedroom to play around with the guitar. Under threat of the whipping to end all whippings, the boy played. He played so well, in fact, that this time at least, he was able to escape the dreaded spanking.

Jackson was too busy thinking to spank. He was too busy seeing with new eyes that which had been under his nose all along. The boys were always singing around the house—mainly harmonizing on such oldies as "Cotton Fields" and "Down In The Valley" for the amusement of their folks. But the Jackson patriarch wasn't seeing amusement the day his third child played the guitar for him. He was seeing an old and cherished dream which, perhaps, wasn't as dead as he had thought.

Papa Joe gathered his three oldest boys—Sigmund, Tito and Jermaine—and started working with them, teaching them the basics. Michael and Marlon were toddlers at the time, hardly old enough to participate with the older boys. Papa Joe liked the sounds he was getting out of his three older boys, as the girls—Maureen and LaToya—accompanied them on violin and clarinet.

The impromptu rehearsals continued. As soon as they were old enough, Michael and Marlon were added to the group. Jermaine, who had handled lead vocals for the Jackson trio, soon found himself playing second-banana to his four-year-old brother, Michael. Michael was developing rapidly into a tiny, apple-cheeked dynamo. He exploded all over the place in a dazzling, pyrotechnic display of dancing and singing influenced in large part by soul superstar James Brown. Joe knew he had something big on his hands.

As he told *Rolling Stone* in 1971, "We went overboard. My wife and I would fight, because I invested in new instruments that cost so much. When a woman's a good mother and finds all the money going into instruments, she doesn't like it." But for that moment, at

A proud dad joins his sons and baby girl Janet.

When the Jackson 5 first got started, they made frequent appearances on television on such shows as *Ed Sullivan, Flip Wilson* and from time to time, had their own specials. Michael, of course, was a standout.

least, what Katherine Jackson liked or didn't like was immaterial. Joe Jackson was pumped up on his dream, perhaps seeing himself in the eyes of the five little boys who performed with a dizzying professionalism far beyond their tender years.

There was, of course, a price to be paid for that professionalism. The boys spent many long, hard hours in the small house at 23rd and (ironically enough) Jackson streets, rehearsing under Papa Joe's stern eye. As Tito told the *Los Angeles Times* in 1981, "The other kids would pass by our house on the way home from school and they'd see us practicing everyday. Some of them stopped to listen. Others would make fun. They'd say, 'Look at those Jacksons. They won't get anywhere. They're just doing all that for nothing.'"

In a 1977 *Times* interview, Michael said, "It's kind of a shame we couldn't grow up doing what the other kids did. We had to rehearse everyday after school when the other kids were outside playing. Sometimes we could hear all the fun and excitement but we could never join in. We missed trick-or-treating and football games and all that. Sure, we had plenty of things the other kids didn't have, but we had to sacrifice to get those things."

In 1965, 7-year-old Michael went onstage for the first time with his brothers. The occasion was a talent show at a local high school. The Jackson 5 sang a current hit, the Temptations' now-classic "My Girl" and walked off with first prize. It was only the first of a handful of first-place awards the Jackson 5 were to collect over the next two years.

"I was scared, of course," Michael has said of those early days. "I was scared to let the people see me sing. They might 'boo' us. They might not like us. But I've never been so scared that I wasn't ready . . . never worried about forgetting lyrics. I make sure I have it before I do it."

For his part, Papa Joe was seeing his dream

come true before his amazed eyes. "At first, I told myself they were still just kids, that there was plenty of time for a career. But the longer I tried to wait, the better they got. Their music got more complicated and they needed more and more direction all the time. I soon realized that they were very professional. There was nothing to wait for. The boys were ready for stage training and I ran out of reasons to keep them from the school of hard knocks."

Papa Joe began lining up professional jobs for his boys. Initially, the Jackson 5 only performed in and around Gary. Soon, though, Joe got a bit more ambitious. When weekends and school vacations came, the boys and a pair of cousins loaded into a Volkswagen bus, carrying their equipment in a second van, they traveled to gigs in Chicago, Boston, New York and other major cities. Once, Papa Joe drove his brood all the way to Arizona to play a date. The acts the Jackson 5 were opening for back then were among the heavyweights of the day—the Chi Lites, the Temptations, Jackie Wilson, Etta James, the O'Jays, the Emotions, Gladys Knight and the Pips. . . .

Eventually, the Jackson 5 was signed to a recording contract with an obscure local label, Steel Town. The single, "Big Boy" went down quickly. A single on the Mercury label, "You Don't Have To Be 21 To Fall In Love," suffered a similar fate. Tito has since said of those early releases that he and his brothers "just weren't ready" at the time.

They were, however, "ready" by 1968. That's the year Motown came into the picture. Exactly *how* Motown came into the picture is a matter of mystery. Popular legend has it that Diana Ross discovered the Jackson 5 while she was in Gary to attend a benefit for Mayor Richard Hatcher. Actually, the "legend" is more myth than anything else. Gladys Knight and the Pips say they saw the boys first, but, since that family foursome was itself between hits at the time, they lacked the clout necessary to get the right people to give a listen.

Bobby Taylor is the former leader of a now-defunct Motown group called Bobby Taylor and the Vancouvers, whose members once included Thomas Chong of Cheech and Chong fame. Taylor says *he's* the one who discovered

The Jackson Five always found time to shoot a few baskets.

15

Janet's saucy Mae West impersonation won her many fans.

the boys. He recalls entering an arena at the "half"—i.e., one-half hour before his own curtain call—and stopping for a moment to check out the opening act.

Taylor says he was so amazed at what he saw, at this spinning, jumping, pint-sized James Brown and his brothers, that he placed a call to Motown. The result, according to Taylor, was an audition and a signing. He says it was at that point that Motown decided to attach Diana's name to the project; she was a bigger star than Taylor and her sponsorship was likely to draw more attention. Taylor, who is listed among the producers of the Jackson 5's debut album, says the decision didn't bother him in the least.

Michael himself has been quoted as saying that "Nobody discovered the Jacksons except their mother and father." In final analysis, of course, the question of who gets credit for bringing the Jackson brothers to light is irrelevant. The important thing is that they were discovered and signed to Motown. No one has spoken yet about what went on in

the year between Motown's signing of the Jackson 5 and its release of their first record. If the Motor City label was living up to its rep, though, it's safe to assume that that first year was spent in grooming the youngsters, instilling in them the polish and poise they would need to face the fame that seemed imminent.

Some critics have written that the Jackson 5 were the last gasp of the Motown assembly line method of cranking out hits. If that's true, then it's safe to say that method died with a blast. Motown unveiled its newest acquisition privately, at first, showcasing them at the Detroit home of label founder Berry Gordy, Jr. "It was the biggest place we had ever seen," says Jackie. "His backyard was like a golf course and he had an indoor pool. He had us entertain at a party and most of the Motown artists were there. That's what really scared us. We were up there doing *their* songs."

In late August of 1969, the wraps came completely off when Diana Ross hosted a

16

party at the Daisy discotheque in Beverly Hills to introduce to the world this new group she had "discovered." That was also when Motown unleashed "I Want You Back," one of the best 45s to ever hit the streets.

"I Want You Back" takes off like a rocket from a piano glissando and immediately sets a nervous, frenetic pace that never once lets up. The record has been described as having some of the best piano, bass and drum work ever recorded, but what really sets "I Want You Back" apart is its energy. Little Michael is all over the tune like a crazy person, singing in occasionally-hoarse desperation and, in trade-off vocals with Jermaine, belting out some adlibs that would've done James Brown proud. The song is framed by some string work that gives it a peppy, schoolyard innocence but for the astute listener, a single earful of Michael, crying for mercy as if his life depends on it, is enough to dispel any notion that this is child's play.

"I Want You Back," which went to Number One and remains the best Jackon 5 record

ever, was more than just a hit. It was the song that lit the fuse on an exploding phenomenon. Motown's star-making machinery went into overdrive with the success of "I Want You Back" and the result was that soon you couldn't go a day without being confronted with the scrubbed cheeks and chipper smiles of America's sweethearts, the Jackson 5.

You'd never know that America had ever had a problem with racial discrimination the way the nation welcomed the Jackson 5 into its hearts. There had been young stars and national teen heroes before, to be sure, but few of those youngsters were really talented and certainly, none of them were black. But the Jackson brothers, a group of all-American boys if ever there was one, soon made blackness irrelevant.

The group racked up an amazing four Number One pop singles in a row with "I Want You Back," "ABC" (a Grammy winner for Best Pop Song), "The Love You Save" and a gorgeous ballad, "I'll Be There." The

Katherine Jackson steps out with daughters Janet and Latoya.

explosion of the Jackson brothers has been likened to the Beatlemania of less than a decade before and indeed, there is more than a passing similarity.

Fan magazines that had previously only carried articles on the likes of David Cassidy and Bobby Sherman began competing with one another to see which could best satisfy a public that just couldn't get enough of Papa Joe's boys. There was no aspect of their lives insignificant enough to escape notice. Headlines like "Jermaine's Jiving Jeans" and "Marlon and His Tee-Hee Tee Shirts" accompanied articles that gave page after page of such "vital" information as height, weight, shoe size, eye and hair color, hobbies, ambitions, favorite performers, favorite TV programs, etc. for each of the Jacksons.

Perhaps all this attention was backed by the cynical assumption that the Jackson brothers were simply the latest hot act in a music industry that has made here-today-gone-tomorrow a way of life. But the fact is, after all that clamor, fans still came back for more.

Motown, ever on the alert for new promotional opportunities, discovered a goldmine in the Jackson brothers. The company used the inner sleeves of Jackson 5 records to sell "Giant-Sized Photo Posters" and "Personal Soul-Mate Kits" on the boys, along with Jackson 5 photo stickers, a "private" photo album, autographed portraits, an "official" concert poster, a Jackson 5 magazine, stationery and note pads. The group's mail bag swelled as thousands of lovestruck young girls across the country wrote in to profess their undying adoration.

Interviewers who encountered the Jackson 5 invariably reported on their meetings in glowing terms. Far from the spoiled, showbiz brats many had expected to find, those reports spoke of remarkably polite, well-mannered kids who were not in the least moved by what was happening to them. Perhaps that's the way it really was but, in retrospect, it only seems all the more

18

With sis Rebbie in front, Tito hugs wife Dee Dee, on left, and Hazel.

At a command performance for
Her Majesty the Queen
Elizabeth of England, the
Jacksons showed their
versatility and delighted the
Royal audience. They have
been to Great Britain
many times.

improbable. There was just too much
going on.

The first four Jackson hits were soon
augmented by songs like "Mama's Pearl,"
"Goin' Back To Indiana," "Never Can Say
Goodbye" and "Maybe Tomorrow." In 1972,
the boys received commendations from both
houses of Congress for their "contributions to
American Youth" and, later, gave a command
performance for the Queen of England.

It was probably inevitable, given that kind
of build-up, that critics were waiting eagerly
for the Jackson 5 when the group went on
the road. That eagerness was quite a bit like
that of hungry lions waiting to feast on
helpless Christians. Everyone knew, after all,
that no act could live up to the buildup which
had been lavished on the Jackson 5.

For its part, Motown turned the gamble
into an even higher stakes wager with a
decision to send the brothers out as
headliners; that's a decision virtually
unprecedented for a new and untested act.
How did that gamble turn out? Reviews from
the Jackson 5's summer, '71 tour are
instructive.

"Each of the Jackson 5 steps up for a few
words. Tito sums it up: 'We're glad to be
home. There's no place like home.' "

Indeed, he probably was. But so much had
changed. Kids the five had gone to school
with, grown up with, now viewed them as
heroes—gods from the fabled kingdom of
Southern California. *Rolling Stone* again:
"The friend is dressed OK, but he's not in
pink top and Indian rainbow-print slacks with
puffballs down to the bottom of the bell, like
Marlon. He's checking Marlon out, stands
back a little, you know, but Marlon just wants
to find out about all the old friends from
grammar school. . . ."

Most of the critics who reported on the shows were lukewarm on the opening acts and one critic called them a "run of the mill soul ensemble". But the Five were another matter. As *Cashbox* noted, "The J-5 are most definitely an act in the fullest sense of the term. Quite simple and quiet offstage, when they hit the boards they go wild, the crowd goes wild and fury feeds fury."

Interestingly, ex-Commodore Lionel Richie has since recounted how, the first time his band opened for the Jackson 5, the older group held a meeting and decided to go easy

their own.

Television was keeping an interested eye on the fast-developing five as well. From the start, they had been almost a fixture on *Ed Sullivan* and other talk and variety shows. One of their most important early appearances was with Diana Ross, their "discoverer," on her 1971 ABC-TV special with Danny Thomas and Bill Cosby.

For a time, the Jackson 5 were also the stars of their own animated Saturday morning series. Motown produced the series, hiring five young actors to provide the voices of the Jackson brothers, whose only real connection with the show was in providing the music. At the time, the group's cartoon show was viewed as an important break-through in children's television. As one Motown official put it, "The audience, black and white, is going to see black kids on Saturday morning. It isn't going to be all white faces."

But, perhaps the Jackson 5's most important early TV exposure was "Goin' Back To Indiana," a special that aired on the evening of September 19, 1971 on ABC. Guests Bill Cosby, Elgin Baylor, Ben Davidson, Bill Russell, and Tom Smothers joined the five in sports and racing skits. The centerpiece of the evening, though, was, as the title implied, Jackson 5's return to their home state.

The occasion was a triumphant pair of benefit concerts to aid the re-election campaign of Mayor Richard Hatcher. *Rolling Stone*'s Ben Fong-Torres reported on the welcoming ceremonies at City Hall. "The Jackson 5 go through it all with consummate grace. They accept a flag that has flown atop the state capitol, a gift from a Congressman. They get a plaque from Indiana University, for inspiring 'hope in the young.' Mayor Hatcher himself presents plaqued keys from his city, "so proud, today, that the Jackson 5 has carried the name of Gary throughout the country and the world and made it a name to be proud of."

on the young whippersnappers. Richie says, immediately after that first show, the Commodores held another meeting at which they decided the Jackson 5 was one group that definitely didn't need Commodore charity. The Commodores had to go back out with both machine guns blazing just to hold

Going Places

The Jackson 5 were flying so high in the early '70s that a crash was, inevitable. The basic problem was that the boys were getting older and what had worked even a year or two before was no longer viable, what with Tito, Jackie and Jermaine looking more and more like men everyday. The *five* were getting older, but their sound was not.

"*Lookin' Through The Window*" was the precursor of the disaster to come. It was, at its core, the same peppy kiddy-pop of previous releases, although one could make a pretty convincing argument that the title track and "Ain't Nothin' Like The Real Thing" pointed toward more mature dimensions for the five. Regardless, the public wasn't buying; the album was only a moderate success in comparison to previous releases. It was, quite obviously, time to revise the five's sound. Instead, Motown, in a rare miscalculation, sunk them deeper into an outdated image.

Things change in the music business with bewildering speed, so those in charge of the group's career cannot be faulted too heavily for failing to correctly interpret the signs of Windows' mediocre performance. When *Skywriter* came along in 1973, they simply turned up the sugar content to an unbearably syrupy high. The result was the group's biggest and only bomb to that date. Although *Skywriter* had its moments (most notably a fine treatment of "Corner Of The Sky" from *Pippin*) it was, in the end, simply a childish, harmless sound that indicated creative stagnation.

The situation didn't last long. The next Jackson 5 album, *Get It Together*, was turned over to veteran producer Hal Davis, who wisely tossed out the restraints and allowed the group room to breathe. *Get It Together* was a fun, funky album that showcased the fact that these were, after all, young men. "Dancin' Machine," from that album, is a Jacksons' classic that went on to become a worldwide best-seller. Although the Jackson 5 released a couple of other noteworthy Motown albums (*I Am Love*, *Moving Violation*), *Get It Together* and its high single were the group's last great moment of commercial success on the Detroit label.

By 1974, however, there was evidence that the Jackson 5 was already looking beyond hit records anyway. The traditional Motown wisdom has it, that it makes no sense for an act to restrict itself to record sales in the youth or black markets, when there's so much money to be made in establishing widespread crossover appeal. In a move reflective of that philosophy, the Jackson 5 took its act to Las Vegas in early 1974.

The brothers prepared a special act for the Sin capital, an act apparently influenced by a desire to prove themselves, once and for all, not just a kiddie act. Thus, the Vegas show was more of a Jackson family revue than a Jackson 5 concert. Young Randy and Janet offered devastatingly on-target impressions of Sonny and Cher and Jeanette MacDonald and Nelson Eddy. Seventeen-year-old LaToya joined her brothers for an intricate tap dance routine, and the five augmented their regular repertoire with impressions of such past acts as the Mills Brothers and the Four Freshmen.

26

Las Vegas was impressed. So much so, in fact, that the group was invited back to the *Celebrity Room* of the MGM Grand Hotel the very next year.

"We knew Las Vegas would be different from previous engagements," Jackie said afterward, "but we weren't prepared for the total silence. We were used to screaming girls and concert audiences hollerin' and stompin' their feet. The Las Vegas crowd seemed to be saying, 'show me.' For a split second we were frightened, but then that magic that exisits

between a performer and an audience came into play. They liked us and we liked them."

Indulgent parents whose kids had dragged them to Las Vegas from as far away as Chicago pronounced themselves impressed by the sons and daughters of Joe and Katherine Jackson. Many observers took it upon themselves to anoint the Jacksons as the hottest new attraction in Vegas. It seemed pretty apparent that Motown had established another beachhead in its upward climb.

On Monday, June 30th, 1975, the Jackson 5

dropped a bomb they had apparently been preparing for quite some time. That morning's *Hollywood Reporter* carried an ominous headline: "Motown Denies Jackson Five On Way To Epic Discs." Translated to English, that means: "Motown Denies The Jackson Five Have Signed a Contract With Epic." In the body of the story, Motown vice-chairman Mike Roshkind denied rumors that the Jackson 5 was leaving his label for a home at the giant CBS-owned company. But, he allowed that, "There may be substance to the reports that Epic has talked to the group or that *some* of them have signed to go over to Epic at the termination of Motown's contract."

Later on the day that story appeared, the Jackson 5 confirmed it. In a press conference in New York City, the group announced that it was ending its association with Motown, effective after the next album. From that announcement, the storm broke loose, a lengthy dance of charge and countercharge.

Papa Joe Jackson, who had once praised Motown for treating the boys "like a second set of parents," now accused the company of stifling his boys' creativity. He said Motown discouraged the boys from attempting to write or produce their own material, preferring to think of them simply as singers and performers. In a *Soul* magazine report, Jackson complained that "Everytime I went in there, trying to get them to do something, they said, 'Oh, the J-5 aren't writers and producers, they're entertainers.' I just don't want them to be like some of the other groups. I want them to be able to utilize all their talent. I want the people in the world to know that they can do other things than just getting onstage."

For its part, Motown clung with a jealous passion to the name, the Jackson 5, defending to the death in several published reports their intention to keep the group from recording under that title for any other label. For a time, there was confusion over just what the group would be called. There was also confusion over the status of the brother in the middle, Jermaine. Jermaine, who had married the daughter of Motown's Berry Gordy (see Jermaine chapter) was the wild card in the deck.

Motown steadfastly claimed that Jermaine had not and would not follow his brothers over to Epic. Epic's negotiators, continued to express unflagging optimism that they would be able to reach a deal with Jermaine shortly. The Jackson family publicly, kept its fingers crossed that Jermaine would join his brothers, and issued conciliatory statements indicating that the door for such a move remained wide open. But they had, it seems, reckoned without Jermaine's stubbornness. To paraphrase the old gospel standard, despite their best arguments, he would not be moved.

Motown, meanwhile, was not inclined to let go of the other brothers without a fight. Then-president Ewart Abner accused the group of breaching good faith in signing the Epic deal. He was quoted in *Soul* as saying Motown was never offered the opportunity to fight for one of its most important acts. "There was an agreement whereby they were free to go and get an offer and then Motown would have the right to match it. If we did, they would remain at Motown. Unfortunately, that did not happen. . . . I was aware of the rumors that they were talking to other recording companies. It didn't bother me because the understanding with Joe was that whatever kind of offer he got, all we had to do was match it and they would stay home. Even though they did their shopping, they never gave us an opportunity to match the offer."

The loss of the Jackson brothers was a blow for which Motown seemed unprepared and ill-equiped to deal with. For awhile, as the flurry of charges swirled, the label was like a punch-drunk old boxer, reacting to instead of acting upon, living life on the defensive.

There was some legal action aimed at impeding the group's move, but court rulings tended to favor the group and the issue of what the group would henceforth be called turned out not to be such a roadblock after

31

all. The Jackson 5 became, simply, the Jacksons. Motown released *Joyful Jukebox Music*, a last album of the Jackson 5; it died quickly and without notice.

While Motown's wounds were slowly closing, the Jacksons took their act to television in a half-hour variety show. The show, which had its debut as a summer replacement series, was picked up by the network as a regular season series, but it didn't last long. Despite what were reported to be good ratings, the show's plug was inexplicably pulled. While *The Jacksons* lasted, however, it was a fast-paced 30 minutes of television. The group usually opened and closed each show with a song from its repertoire, leaving the minutes in-between for comedy sketches and dance numbers that often included sisters Janet, Maureen and LaToya. The presence of the sisters helped the group to bring into the living room of America a side of the Jacksons that had theretofore been seen only on the Las Vegas stage.

Epic Records didn't release its first album on the Jacksons immediately, apparently preferring to hold off and use caution. However, as the summer of 1976 got underway, the lack of any new Jackson product in the streets only helped fuel the simmering controversy over the group's departure from Motown. It had been a year since the announcement in New York that they were leaving that label, but time apparently did little to calm emotions.

The legal assaults continued, with the Jacksons finally countersuing and claiming that Motown had withheld some royalties. Motown executives issued increasingly angry statements on the Jacksons, while some observers criticized the brothers for "selling out" a black company for a white one. A *Sepia* magazine account quotes Jackie as hoping "black people will understand we're moving onto better things. I hope black people will understand that the Jacksons didn't leave Motown for nothing. I hope no one plays on that black stuff."

Even Katherine Jackson, the quiet, reserved matriarch of the clan, got into the act, declaring that "I just hope Motown has finally learned to let go of my boys. The way Motown was acting, it's like a mother holding onto a child and saying, 'I raised you, so you owe me your life!' There has to be a time to let go, in a family or in a business. Motown wouldn't have signed the boys in the first place if they didn't think their talents could do the company some good. Sure, we appreciate the things Motown did for the boys. But we also hope they appreciate what the boys did for them."

And on the subject of the prodigal son Jermaine, the comments, though still conciliatory, were occasionally tinged by the anger of the times. Papa Joe told *Sepia*, "It's my blood that flows through his body—not Gordy's. Jermaine has a lot of people talking to him on the other side, so it's difficult for him to come back."

Finally, passions were allowed to cool somewhat with the release of *The Jacksons*, the group's debut album for Epic. The boys were teamed with producers Kenny Gamble and Leon Huff, who were then having great success with *Sounds of Philadelphia* hits crafted for such artists as Harold Melvin and the Bluenotes and the O'Jays. Under Gamble and Huff's aegis, the Jackson style began to grow up and to mature for the first time since "Get It Together" in 1973. The perky "Enjoy Yourself" and a tune called "Show You The Way To Go" were the most popular tunes from that album, but the Jacksons had yet to rival the popularity of their best Motown work. There were, however, two tunes on the album (*Blues Away* and *Style of Life*) that were written and co-produced by the Jacksons.

The group's next album, *Goin' Places*, was also a Gamble and Huff production that, like its predecessor, featured a pair of Jackson-written and Jackson-produced tunes. Also like it predecessor, *Goin' Places* was more adult than previous Jackson efforts, moving along

under power of stylized Philly orchestrations. The only problem with *Goin' Places*, actually, was that it didn't sell.

It was 1978 before the Jacksons got what they had left Motown for—a chance to write and perform their albums in their entirety. The result was *Destiny*, which, with its smash single, "Shake Your Body (Down To The Ground)," put the brothers firmly back on the hit records track from which they had been away too long.

On *Destiny*, the Jacksons did what a horde of stellar writers and producers had been unwilling or unable to do. They brought their music all the way within the realm of grown-up sound, distancing themselves finally and irrevocably from such gems as "I Want You Back" and "ABC." They were grown men now and it was time to start acting like it.

The *Destiny* album offers an essentially spare, stripped down sound that's miles away from the gaudiness of some of the early hits.

That tact was repeated in the group's 1980 hit album, *Triumph*, with its hit single, "Lovely One."

The success of *Destiny* was with a big promotion by Epic in celebration of the group's 10th year of hits. The Jackson were subjected to some of the most intense media attention they had had to that date. *Billboard* magazine put together a special issue in honor of the group and press from around the world kept hammering at them with essentially the same question: What does it feel like to come of age and to write and produce your own music? Marlon answered the question in *Billboard*. "The past," he said, "has been producers producing the Jacksons, writing songs for the Jacksons, which we sang, we did the best we could, and at which we were very successful. But this is the Jacksons' music. This is the way we hear music."

The tenth anniversary celebration was

33

Michael's popularity is evident by this now-famous photo. Ten thousand screaming fans waited below for a glimpse of the young performer in Tennessee. At the time, Michael was doing *The Wiz* in which he starred with Diana Ross. Michael now requires more security guards to travel with him.

capped with a lavish party in a Beverly Hills bank, which had been specially-equipped with a dance floor just for the occasion. Party guests—Southern California's so-called "beautiful people"—sipped champagne and munched hor d'oeuvres as they waited for the guests of honor. When the Jacksons arrived, they made an entrance as dramatic as any they ever did onstage. As giant, house-rocking speakers pumped out the frenzied rhythms of "I Want You Back," the entire Jackson family descended by escalator into a room full of cheering, applauding well-wishers.

If there was a bittersweet note to the

celebration, it was certainly in the ten-years-ago voice that poured out of the speakers in harmony with the others, occasionally challenging brother Michael in spirited adlibs. Jermaine applauded his brothers in a comment made in *Billboard*, but he didn't appear at the party. That Jermaine was such a phantom presence at a celebration of a sound he helped create was sad, but if that thought was in the minds of the Jacksons and their guests that afternoon, they didn't show it. They were all too busy dancing to the music, lifting their glasses to toast a dream.

A Mean Guitarist

TITO "Toro," the word from which Toriano Adaryll "Tito" Jackson gets his name, is Spanish for bull. It's not often one encounters a name that so aptly fits its bearer. Tito Jackson is built somewhat like a bull; he's a compact, almost stocky young man who looks as if he could stand his ground in a hurricane if he set his mind to it.

Tito also resembles his namesake in terms of single-minded self-confidence. He sets his mind on something and apparently he does it (or tries to), regardless of odds or counter opinions. Unlike brother Michael, who has become a virtual prisoner of his own fame, Tito seems to have remained highly unaffected by the phenomenon in which he grew up. In the summer of '82, he was spotted standing near the front gate of a Temptations concert, dressed casually in short pants and shirt. Far from ducking his fans, he stood there in their midst as one of them . . . just another music lover going to see the Tempts, and, because it's human nature to ignore that which is right under one's nose, many fans didn't even give him a second look.

Tito is an antique car buff who has been described in more than one press account as a mechanical-minded man. One of the characteristics of most mechanical-minded folks is their inability to rest until they figure out how every thingamabob and whatchamacallit works. Again, there's a bull-like stubbornness in that which one must note—and admire.

Presumably, it was that kind of stubbornness which made Tito sneak into his father's bedroom as a child and pull down Papa Joe's prized guitar. Tito snuck the instrument out time and time again, knowing full well the kind of punishment his stern father could administer if he found out what was going on. But Tito learned to play the guitar, so well, in fact, that when Papa Joe found out what was going on and told his son to play the music or face the music, Tito was able to escape with his rear end intact.

Many people thought Tito was too young to know what he was doing when, at 18, he married his high school sweetheart, the

Right: Tito Jackson married his high school sweetheart Dee Dee, who was referred by the media as "the little bitty pretty one." The couple have three sons, Taj, Tarryl and Tito Joe. Notice, they all begin with a "T"? That's no coincidence!

Far right: Tito's favorite hobby is playing softball and he's the one who organizes the group's celebrity games against disc jockeys.

For Tito's 25th birthday, Dee Dee surprised him with a barbecue picnic and a brand-new Rolls-Royce. He was delighted by the treat. Many celebrities stopped by to congratulate him.

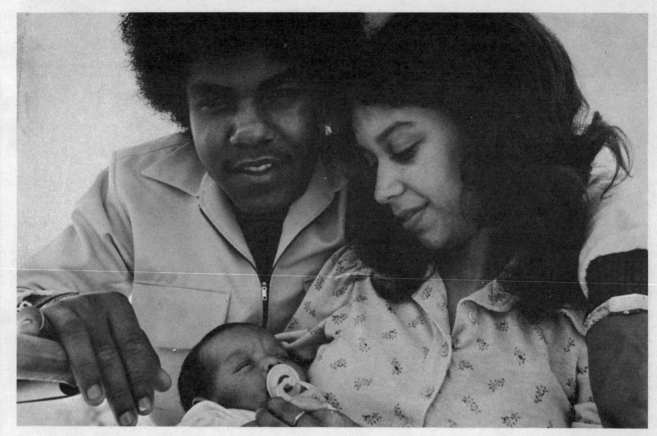

Tito and his wife Dee Dee were first parents of Taj, a darling boy.

Lionel Richie, Jr. has always admired the Jacksons since the Commodores opened shows for the group.

Dee Dee enjoys being a mommy to the boys. Tarryl, Tito and Taj keep her busy.

former Delores Martes. It was a marriage they said couldn't last—but it did, in spite of Tito's occasionally male chavinistic outlook. "I'm the man of the house," he told *Soul* in 1973. "For sure. Gots to be, or else I'll be walking the street in a dress."

Rolling Stone pegged Tito as the "toughest" looking of the Jackson brothers. *Soul*'s Naomi Rubine pictured him a tad more accurately. "If you could describe this young man with one word, it would probably be self-assured. His manner, his choice of words, the inflection in his voice—all these add to the image of a boy who has just passed over the brink into manhood. Instead of sitting meekly in his

chair, he leans it back on its hind legs, like a movie executive sizing things up before asserting his authority."

Although the flip side of self-assuredness is close mindedness, Tito is something of a refreshing change of pace in a world where opinions and goals shift faster than newspaper headlines. Still, even the bull-like Tito hasn't been able to have things totally his way. In 1972, he mentioned to a reporter that he was going to get involved in acting and film production. Although that Tito Jackson goal has yet to reach fruition, Joe Jackson's second son seems to be very much satisfied with the current shape of his life.

41

The Daring Conga Player

RANDY Steven Randall "Randy" Jackson lived on the periphery. Magazine writers would sometimes speculate, in the early days of the Jackson 5, about how Joe Jackson had another player warming up in the bullpen, so to speak. Other writers would dutifully report only that he was at home, growing up in the limelight with baby sister Janet.

Even when Randy joined the group, he was treated often as an afterthought. Perhaps promoters and record company executives were jittery about confusing the public by tampering with a well-known logo; whatever the reason, Randy's presence was never acknowledged by a changing of the numerical portion of the group's name. In an unfathomable bit of mathematic wizardry, pictures of all six Jackson sons were still labeled "The Jackson *Five*," which must have left some poor, unaware souls scratching their heads in confusion. Similarly, although Randy reportedly joined his brothers in recording sessions in the early '70s, no mention of such a contribution was ever made on the liner notes (Motown albums have long been notorious for not listing the players) and his picture didn't appear on the albums.

It was only when Jermaine left the group and Randy "officially" joined his brothers that his name and face began to appear on albums and in press material. Randy, a happy-go-lucky soul who appeared to be proud enough of just joining his big brothers, never mumbled even a word of complaint.

On March 3rd, 1980, Randy came to public attention in a tragic way. Randy, who was then 19, was driving his Mercedes along a slippery, rain-soaked Hollywood street when he lost control of the vehicle and slammed into a utility pole. Randy was trapped in the car for over half an hour before rescuers were able to pry him loose using a "Jaws Of Life."

The young man they pulled out of the wreckage had sustained severe fractures of both ankles and his left foot. Initially, doctors thought they might have to amputate both of his legs. Eventually, that dire diagnosis was

Punk rocker Randy scared the
living daylights out of his family
when he had a severe auto
crash which caused temporary
paralysis. It was feared he'd
never walk again, but
comedian Dick Gregory gave
him courage and inspiration
to try.

44

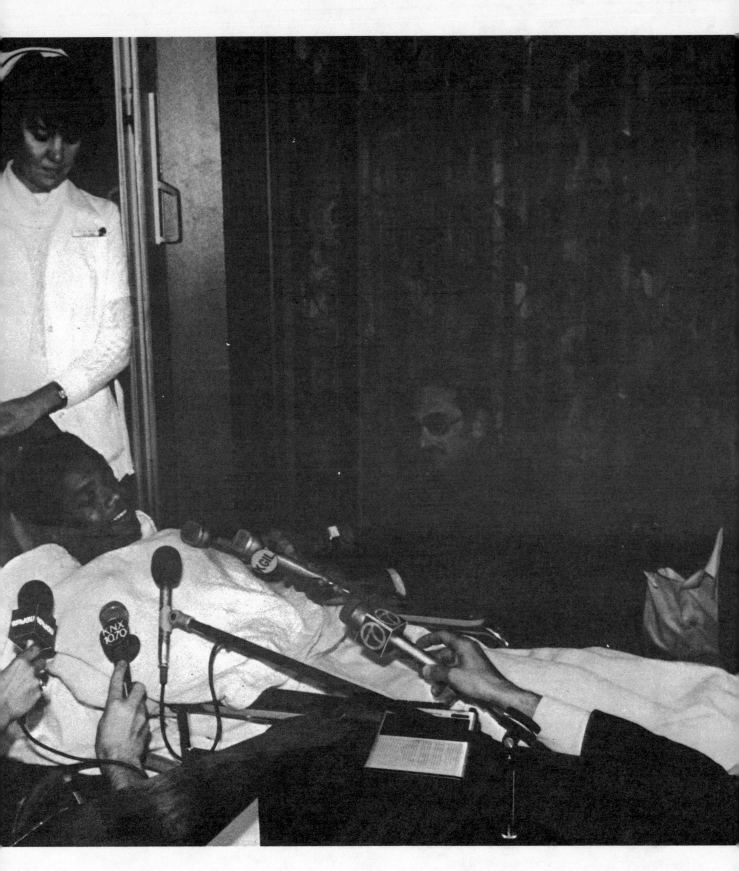

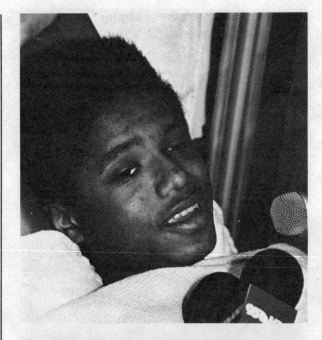

modified to something only relatively less devastating. They told him he would never walk again. That's when Randy showed what he was made of.

In a press conference at St. Joseph's Medical Center in Burbank, Randy vowed that it was just a "matter of time" before he would return to work. That vow, unfortunately, carried a hollow ring because it was one of many such promises, made by many people who still today are confined to their wheelchairs.

But Randy not only made the vow; he flat-out rejected the medical diagnosis. "I never even thought about the worst," he told the *Los Angeles Times*. "I was laughing as soon as the doctors left the room. I refused to accept it. When my mom and brothers started crying in the hospital room, I told them to go away if they were going to act like that. As soon as the cast came off, I started doing therapy. I knew I'd soon be back onstage."

The very next year, he was.

Dapper And Dazzling

MARLON Katherine Jackson once described her son Marlon David as the "sweetest" of her boys and one who gets offended most easily. If it's true that Marlon is easily offended, he may well have had a miserable time of it back in the early days of the Jackson 5. Marlon and Michael are close in age—barely a year a half apart (Marlon's the oldest) and thus, it was natural that the two of them would be best buddies in the insular world in which they lived. It was natural, also, that outsiders, in sizing up the group, would compare the two.

The problem with that is that Michael is a light which, instead of illuminating, casts shadows. Marlon grew up in those shadows, always being known as Michael's best friend and closest brother, but rarely being acknowledged as a whole and talented person in his own right.

It took years for Marlon to grow out of that shadow and assert himself as something other than an appendage of Michael. That's ironic, because right from the beginning, Marlon's contributions to the Jackson 5 were apparent to anyone who cared enough to do some investigation. As a few early Jackson 5 articles noted, Marlon was and is an excellent dancer; it was he who took responsibility for working out many of the group's intricate dance routines. And there's another which did not come to light until after Jermaine left the group—Marlon is an excellent vocalist. He has taken over most of Jermaine's lead vocals in the groups repertoire and has proven himself a singer of stylish, gutbucket soul instincts.

Being out of the spotlight, though, has allowed Marlon, like some of the other brothers, to move on the periphery without always being noticed right away. Case in point: In mid-August of 1975 Marlon, who was then 18, married his longtime sweetheart, the former Carol Parker. Marlon, for some unknown reason, wanted to keep the nuptials secret. He succeeded—so well, in fact, that when reporters attempted to verify the wedding four months after it had taken place, even Joe Jackson didn't know for sure.

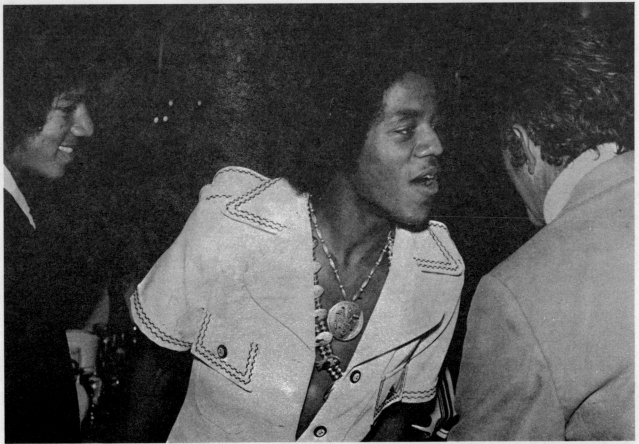

Dean Martin greets members of the Jackson Five at a Paul McCartney party aboard the luxurious Queen Mary.

Marlon is no
longer a sexy, eligible bachelor,
but husband of budding model
Carol P. Jackson, two beautiful
daughters and a son. Marlon
likes to wear buttons on which
he laminates photos of his
children.

Always a snazzy dresser, Marlon has loved hats since he was small. His grooming is impeccable.

"Marlon didn't tell me he had gotten married," he said. "I've been hearing it 'round and about from other sources, but he didn't tell me.

"What can I say? He may be and he may not. I don't know, but I hear a lot of things. If I start to investigate this, I may find the type of answers that I'm not ready to accept." The answers Papa Joe alluded to had to do with widely-circulated rumors that Carol was pregnant at the time of her marriage. However, she and Marlon had been married for well over a year when she gave birth. They are now the parents of two daughters and a son.

It seems that Marlon has forever been something of an enigma—an unknown factor, even to those who know him best. As Tito told a fan magazine reporter some years ago, "I think Marlon is quiet sometimes because he's thinking about something that's personally very important to him. It could be something to do with something new he's planning for our act, a new dance step, or even a song he may plan to write. Whatever it is, he doesn't talk about it until he's thought it through."

To which Jermaine added, "When you get to spend some time with us, you'll see what I mean when I say that sometimes Marlon is the quiet J-5. Many times I've asked him why, but he only smiles wisely and never answers one word. I've lived with him all his life and I still haven't figured him out."

Soulful And Sexy

JACKIE Sigmund Esco "Jackie" Jackson is proof that at least one of Joe Jackson's children wasn't bound and determined to become a singer from the moment he made his first sounds. Actually, Jackie, the oldest of the Jackson boys had his sights set on a career in sports and remains to this day a big fan of athletic events. As he saw it back then, the rigors of rehearsals and shows cut too deeply into his play time.

In a 1982 interview with *Right On!*, Jackie said that "At the same time we were rehearsing and doing shows, I was trying to pursue a baseball career. I had people watching me play short stop and I was hoping for a professional career."

Of course, he got the professional career, even if it wasn't in the field he would have picked for himself. When the Jackson 5 exploded on the scene, Jackie's dreams of a career in sports were shoved onto a permanent back burner. What he got instead wasn't all that bad, though; he's spent a good part of his life as one-fifth of one of the world's most popular singing groups.

On the other hand, being one-fifth of the total five hasn't been any bed of roses, either. In the early days, when interviewers were pinching Michael's cheeks, and stumbling all over themselves in the effort to find adjectives to properly convey how cute the younger brothers were, Jackie and Tito appeared to get lost a bit in the shuffle.

Jackie, with his high, thin voice and shy, deferential manner, was tailor-made to live life in the background behind his younger brothers. Press people who came to interview the boys invariably painted him as the more mature big brother—too old for boyhood, too young for manhood, the one who kept the rambunctious Michael and Marlon in line and mindful of the fact that work came before play.

In retrospect, it seems that that portrayal wasn't that far off target. Joe Jackson once said of his second child, "If they're rehearsing for a show or something, he wants everything to be perfect. Onstage, he wants everything

Jackie's a hit on the basketball court. They say if he hadn't become part of the Jacksons, he probably would have opted for a career in professional sports. Now, he sits on the sidelines and admires other pros from afar.

57

perfect."

Ben Fong-Torres of *Rolling Stone* put it best. "Sometimes he looks out of place, his high cheekbones drawing his soft features into a just-about adult face. Sometimes, his role appears to be that of puppeteer, letting Marlon and Michael go only so far."

You can count on one hand the times that Jackie—sans group—has made headlines. In early 1972, just before his 21st birthday, Jackie allegedly lost control of his beloved Datsun 240Z sports car and plowed into a parked car at 50 mph. He escaped injury, but his concerned father forbade him to buy another sports car.

A bit over two years later—November 24th, 1974—Jackie married the former Enid Spann in an unassuming ceremony in Las Vegas. Jackie, who had dated Enid for about five years, is said to have foregone the usual wedding formalities, taking his vows in jeans and tennis shoes. The marriage surprised observers, who had assumed that Jackie would be walking the aisle anyday with Debracca Foxx, the daughter of comedian Redd Foxx.

Many of those selfsame observers were probably maliciously gratified when, almost before the wedding cake was digested, Enid turned around and filed for divorce. The

newlyweds reconciled, however, and apparently found wedded bliss. Enid busies herself with Jazbo, her boutique in Los Angeles, which designs stage outfits for Jackie and his famous family among others. They have a son and daughter.

Finally, there was one other time that Jackie came to public attention—luridly. In early 1977, he was arrested by California Highway Patrol officers for allegedly attempting to leave the scene after being pulled over for speeding. When he was told he was under arrest, Jackie allegedly began to struggle and resist arrest. No one was injured in the alleged altercation and the whole incident eventually came to naught.

Life in the shadows can't be the most flattering thing in the world but, as more than one background singer notes, it takes a special kind of talent to support a star, make that star look good, without being obtrusive. And Jackie himself doesn't appear to be losing any sleep over living out of the limelight. As he once told *Right On!*, of the old days, "Everybody was looking at the younger guys, I guess. Maybe I'm wrong. But I didn't care; I was just happy being in the group. It's different now because everybody's the same size so they look as old as I do. Now it's my turn."

Standing On The Top

JERMAINE A writer once called Jermaine the "lamb" of the Jackson family and certainly, the description must have seemed fitting at the time. Jermaine, the middle son and sometimes lead singer of the group, was famed for both his huge, perfect Afro and his wide-open, couldn't-harm-a-fly smile. Female fans who were a little too old to get seriously worked up over Michael found him a convenient fantasy to latch on to. Jermaine was never quite as popular as Michael within the group (no one was), but he carried enough of a following for his *Jermaine* and *Come Into My Life* albums to be strong sellers. A remake of rock 'n' roll oldie "Daddy's Home" remains Jermaine's only solid solo hit from the Jackson 5 days.

Motown capitalized on Jermaine's popularity with a campaign designed to establish him as America's first black teen sex symbol (Mike, after all, was a little young to be considered a *sex* symbol at the time). Whether that campaign worked or not is debatable at best, but Jermaine went along with the whole thing without complaining, even though he didn't really seem to have his heart in it. As he said at the time, "A sex symbol? I'm not a sex symbol. . . . A lot of people say that. Maybe it's the clothes I wear, or one special outfit. I don't know. I just try to be myself."

In 1973, Jermaine told writer Naomi Rubine that, although he was one of the richest and most famous 18-year-olds in the world at the time there was something missing. "I'm happy," he said, "but I'm not *happy* happy. I'm only fair happy. I don't know why, exactly. I can't tell what's missing, 'cause it hasn't come yet. But something's missing. A lot's missing."

Presumably, Jermaine filled that void in his life on December 13th of that same year when he married Hazel Joy Gordy, the only daughter of Motown founder Berry Gordy, Jr. The wedding was widely touted as the poshest nuptials in entertainment history. Motown took over the Beverly Hills hotel for a lavish caviar and champagne affair that reportedly cost Berry Gordy in the neighborhood of $200 thousand dollars. Over 500 invited guests attended the affair, including Los Angeles Mayor and Mrs. Tom Bradley, Diana Ross, Lola Falana and Diahann Carroll.

Smokey Robinson composed and sang a song ("Wedding Song") especially for Jermaine and Hazel. Jermaine waited at the altar, immaculate in a white tux, for Berry Gordy to escort his only daughter to the front. Hazel wore a white satin princess dress with a 12-foot mink-lined train decorated by 75 hundred handsewn pearls. When Hazel got married, Gordy gave new meaning to the words, "money is no object."

It was ironic that Jermaine's beautiful wedding became the focal point of ugly speculation and controversy just two years later. In retrospect, it seems astonishing that no one asked what problems might arise if Jermaine, now that he had married into the Motown clan, were ever pressured to leave the Motown label.

That, of course, is what happened when the Jacksons pulled up stakes. The split was bitter enough on its own dubious merits, as both sides sent charges and countercharges flying through the media. But Jermaine made the matter even more unpredictable by the mere fact of his marriage inside the company. He has claimed repeatedly and emphatically that being married to Berry Gordy's daughter was not the decisive factor in his decision to rebel against the group when they decided to leave Motown. According to Jermaine, since Motown "made me and my brothers what we are," leaving didn't seem right. As he saw and still sees it, nobody could promote the Jacksons like Motown could.

Jermaine says he came to his decision on his own, after being assured by Hazel that the fate of his marriage didn't rest on what he decided. According to Jermaine, his father

62

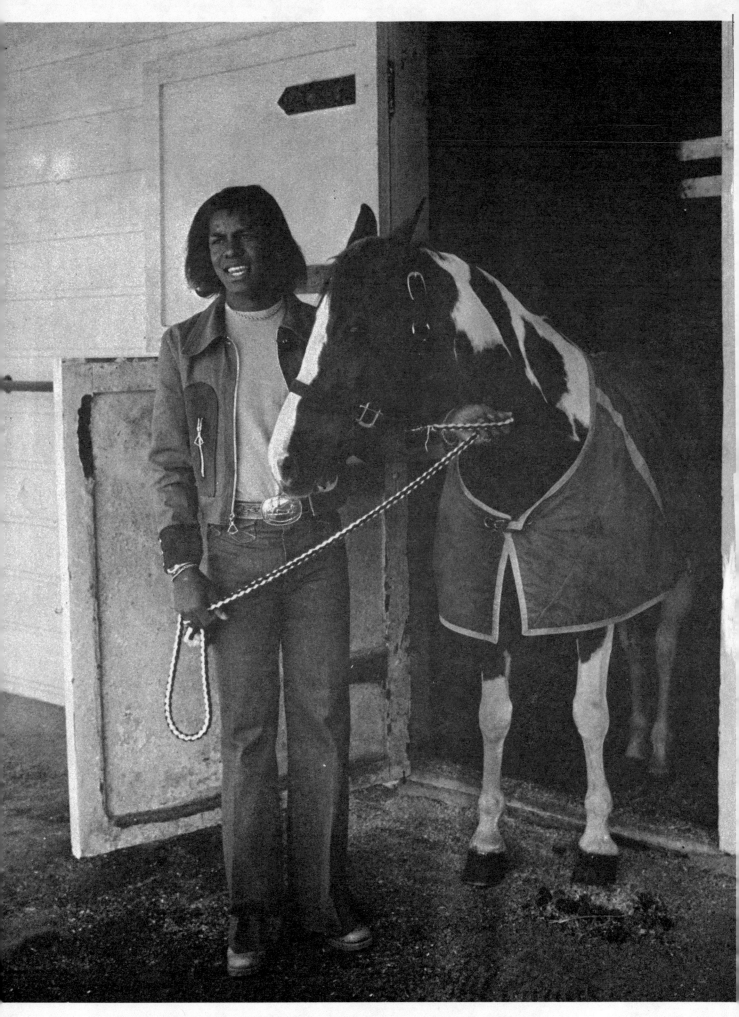

Jermaine loves horses and has a ranch of thoroughbreds which are stabled in an exclusive ranch in Southern California

Jermaine became engaged to Motown President Berry Gordy, Jr.'s only daughter Hazel Joy. They have two children.

wasn't nearly as understanding. He told the *L.A. Times* in 1980 that Papa Joe regarded him as an enemy when the decision to move was made.

"I came home from fishing with my friend Barry White," he said, "and my father called me to come over without Hazel. I knew something was going on. She's a very strong person and she asks a lot of questions. I'm sure my father thought he could get me to do what he wanted if she wasn't there.

"I went to his room and on his bed were the CBS Records contracts. That was the first I knew about it. That was the wrong way to find out. Since I was married to Hazel, they thought they couldn't trust me, so they kept me in the dark. Everybody had signed the contracts. My father picked up mine and said, 'Sign it.' I said, 'No.' "

From that came a split that was nothing less than heartbreaking to a multitude of fans who had always praised the Jackson brothers for being such a tight-knit bunch. The other five brothers, along with the group's fans, accused Jermaine of betraying the family. Mother Katherine questioned her child in print. Jemaine, at the time, put the split in deceptively simply terms: "I just made my choice, they made theirs."

Motown, stung by Jackson family defection, went to work almost immediately on a campaign designed to make Jermaine at least

The celebrated wedding cost over $200,000 and celebrities such as Diana Ross and Smokey Robinson attended.

as big a name as the Jackson 5 had ever been. There were numerous press releases and even a highly-touted free concert. His solo debut, *My Name Is Jermaine* album was whispered before its release to be a self-written and self-produced project (it turned out to be neither) and all the signs seemed to indicate that there were big things in the offing for Jermaine.

Except for one slight problem, that Jermaine couldn't get a hit record. New singles and albums came with regularity and, just as predictably died without ever getting off the ground. The fact that Jermaine's solo career was proving such a high-visibility flop was an embarrassment exacerbated by the fact that his brothers were enjoying such high-visibility success at their new label.

According to some published reports, it got to the point that Berry Gordy cajoled Stevie Wonder into co-producing the *Let's Get Serious* album with Jermaine. The result was, of course, a smash hit single and Grammy nominations. Jermaine's solo career suddenly seemed a viable idea once again. For his part, Jermaine told writers that working with Stevie, the renowned perfectionist, had been an education and he vowed to use what he had learned in upcoming albums. After *Serious*, he was able to produce hit records of respectable proportions for himself, but still found it hard to top the monster disc

that had resurged his career.

When one comes from a family that has been as close as the Jacksons, being considered a traitor by that family is probably a difficult pill to swallow, Jermaine, the father of a son and a daughter, told the *L.A. Times* in 1980 that he swallowed his pride and called his family repeatedly to mend the breach. The brothers, on the other hand, steadfastly claimed in print that although the split existed, it was professional—not personal. They said they still saw and loved Jermaine as much as ever and got together with him whenever possible. That Jermaine chose, in a number of press interviews, to cast doubt on that version of things, to discuss being branded a traitor, is a sign of how deeply Jermaine was really hurt by being an outcast. As he complained in a 1981 *Soul* interview, he doesn't feel that he left his brothers. "We all started here at Motown and if anybody left anybody, I feel they left me."

In the late '70s, as the Jacksons were beginning to enjoy their resurgence, both they and Jermaine were questioned occasionally about the chances of a reunion. The brothers

66

All the Jacksons are favorites of Dick Clark

were generally non-committal, where Jermaine always seemed eager—sadly so—for the reunion. At least twice, he said that such a reunion was definitely in the works, only to have it not take place.

In a *Jet* interview, Jermaine described such a reunion almost as if it were a mission he had set for himself. Jermaine, who did virtually no touring or performing after leaving the Jackson 5, even went so far as to show up at a concert his brothers were giving in Philadelphia. As he told *Soul*, "It felt kind of strange being onstage with them again. I didn't feel as much a part of it as I thought I would. I knew I was still their brother and all, but it was strange."

And that is probably as close as Jermaine Jackson will ever come to an admission that, even though lines of communication have been restored between him and his family, the relationship can never be quite the same as it was before. Somewhere within himself, Jermaine probably recognizes that possibility. But he refuses to accept it. He keeps trying to make things different. And in the end, that's all that really matters.

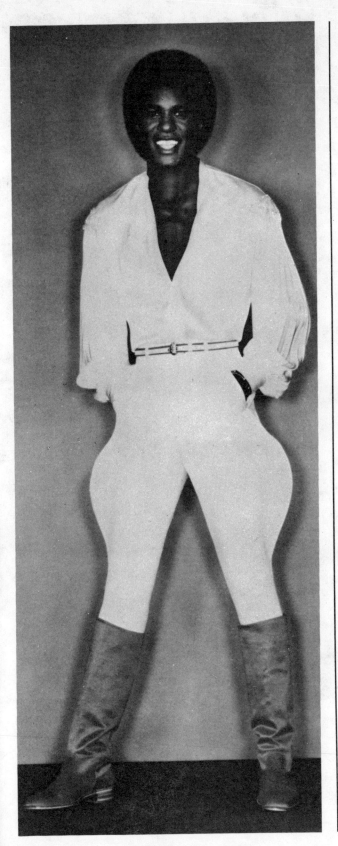

67

exception. He's a frequent Bandstand guest.

A Shining Star

MICHAEL From *Rolling Stone:* "Michael's kindergarten was the basement of the Apollo Theatre in Harlem. He was too shy to actually approach the performers the Jackson Five opened for. But he says he had to know everything they did—how James Brown could do a slide, a spin and a split and still make it back before the mike hit the floor. How the mike itself disappeared through the Apollo stage floor. He crept downstairs, along passageways and walls and hid there, peering from behind the dusty flanks of old vaudeville sets while musicians tuned, smoked, played cards and divided barbecue. Climbing back to the wings, he stood in the protective folds of the musty maroon curtain, watching his favorite acts, committing every double dip and every bump, snap, whip-it-back mike toss, to his inventory of night moves."

The group that would become the Jackson 5 was formed when Michael Jackson was not long out of diapers. Thus, for awhile, he had to content himself with sitting on the sidelines as a spectator, perhaps sensing that his older brothers were into something grown-up and important, without quite knowing what that something was. Jermaine was the lead singer then, and he was surely competent in the job. But it was when Michael himself matured enough to take over that role that the Jackson 5 became something really special.

At first, of course, it was the novelty of seeing such a tiny young boy putting on such an adult performance that drew audiences to the Jackson 5. But somewhere along the way, as Michael grew to manhood but didn't fade from sight, those audiences had to realize that there was something else at work here. That's "something" was talent by the truckloads.

In an industry that lives on its own self-serving hype and the most pitiful performer is the one who believes his own press, it's a good idea to take care not to overstate one's case. Still, that would seem to be a difficult transgression to make in the case of Michael

Jackson. Simply put, he's a once in a lifetime performer.

As Mikal Gilmore of the *Los Angeles Herald-Examiner* put it in one performance review, "Dancing, spinning, sending out impassioned, fierce glares toward the overcome audience, Jackson was simply the single most exciting male pop performer I have ever seen—Frank Sinatra, Bob Dylan, Johnny Rotten, Bruce Springsteen, Mick Jagger, David Bowie and Prince notwithstanding. Like all of those artists, he was confident, cocky and unafraid, but he was also more physically charged and illuminating than even the best of them might hope to be."

Rolling Stone's Gerri Hirshey wrote, "He can tuck his long, thin frame into a figure skater's spin without benefit of ice or skates. Aided by the burn and flash of silvery body suits, he seems to change molecular structure at will, all robot angles one second and rippling curves the next. So sure is the body that his eyes are often closed, his face turned upward to some unseen muse. The bony chest heaves. He pants, bumps and squeals. He has been known to leap offstage and climb up into the rigging."

Michael's performances are an exorcism of sorts, a way of exploding tensions and cares into nothingness. Conversely, those tensions are the basis for all the things that make Michael, Michael.

Observers have called him a young man caught up in the grip of an almost paralyzing shyness. This isn't shyness in the normal sense, where a tied-tongued fellow needs half an hour to work up enough courage to stammer an opening line to a pretty young lady. No, this is the shyness that cripples, that casts shadows over all contacts with other human beings and makes such contact something to be planned with the caution of

a military maneuver and, if possible, avoided altogether.

Michael has often been painted in the press as an innocent in the land of wolves, what one record company executive called "the gentlest spirit" in the music industry. A *Crawdaddy* profile in 1978 had him eating a green salad in a restaurant with his fingers and, wanting to sample some quiche that had been served to someone else at the table, digging into that with his fingers, also. There

is a certain naivete about Michael Jackson which is refreshing in a sense, but quite worrisome also.

John Travolta once starred in a TV movie called *The Boy In The Plastic Bubble*, about a young man with a rare affliction—he had to live in a sealed plastic bubble, because his body lacked normal disease-fighting capacity and even the slightest infection could spell death. When they stormed out of Gary, the Jackson brothers became boys in a plastic bubble, their childhoods interrupted—some would say destroyed—by a self-created phenomenon. Magazine articles dutifully reported on how "normal" the boys were, to the point where they wrote of how the brothers were each dealt a weekly allowance, pending completion of their household chores.

For their part, Joe and Katherine Jackson were simply reacting in a sensible manner to some well-founded fears. And to their credit, the Jackson brothers could have turned out to be spoiled showbiz brats, incapable of dealing with the rest of the world once the house-lights came back on and the auditorium was empty. But on the other hand, there's a certain wistful delusion inherent in talk of how "normal" the boys' childhoods were. There is something profoundly *un*normal about growing up behind an electrified security gate, a gate which turns one's home into a fortress. That atmosphere was underscored by the ominous presence of fearsome guard dogs who patrolled Jackson territory.

It was, as Michael recalls it, a necessary precaution. "There are all kinds of people at our gate," he said. "One lady said she was sent by God; she must see me, or she'll be destroyed. This was a thirty-three-year-old lady. Girls hitchhiking from New York, come in front of our gate and say they wanna stay with us—sleep in. We can't take them in. The neighbors actually take 'em in; they live with our neighbors. There are people out there all the time."

The problem is, a gate which keeps others out also keeps Michael in; it creates a very

73

insular world. Michael has lived in that world for better than half his life. The other brothers outgrew the plastic bubble, perhaps motivated by a need to seek and discover what life was like on the other side of the gate. You can occasionally catch one of them hanging out at a Los Angeles Lakers game or at a concert. They have adjusted well—as well as could be expected—to life as household names.

For Michael, that adjustment simply hasn't happened. In part, that's because as lead voice of the Jacksons, his fame has been more intense than that of his brothers. But there seems to be another reason, too. Something in Michael Jackson has grown familiar, maybe even comfortable within the bubble. He calls the bubble home.

As that situation creates for Michael exaggerated views of the world outside, it also creates for the world outside an unreal view of Michael. And he exists in that tense pull and tug, secure inside the bubble until it's time to go onstage and blow it out. In between those self-exorcisms, he ritualistically goes to his bedroom (he still lives in his parents' home), there to dance himself to exhaustion, until he falls out in what's been described as a laughing, crying sweat.

In quite a few ways, Michael Jackson is a timeless, wondrous innocent—an eternal boy in a man's body and with a superstar's paycheck. The price is high. Inside the bubble, Michael has fashioned for himself a sanctuary, a place where fantasy and reality come together with a peaceful bump, like toys floating in bath water. He talks to writer Gerri Hirshey about building a pirate room in his home, a place of Disneyland Audio Animatronics robot figures in a shootout that would never end.

In 1979, Michael told a writer that he was remodeling the family home in Encino and would build a place that catered to his tastes. The pirate room is one manifestation of that dream. Michael's dream home is also a place of game rooms and state of the art screening

Michael Jackson's ability as a performer is soul stirring. He said he got a lot of his inspiration from watching such veterans as the Temptations and James Brown on television shows. He still enjoys these entertainers today.

rooms. He loves such things, but is too terrified to go "out there" and experience them. Better to bring them inside the bubble.

As he put it in 1979, if you can't go outside, you should have the things you love inside where you can readily get at them. There are, of course, quite a few things that one *has* to go outside for, things that no amount of money can force to fit inside the bubble. Evidently, Michael will cross that bridge when he comes to it.

In the meantime, he enjoys his bubble. On the rare occasions that he ventures tentatively out of it, not a bodyguard in sight, it's a giddy, daring adventure. "I seldom go to movies by myself," he says. "I think I've been once to the movies by myself. I saw "Halloween." I was so scared; it was a scary movie. And I had glasses and a hat and a coat and nobody knew me. I had *such* a good time."

One other thing that can't be made to fit inside the bubble is human companionship.

Michael pals around with the likes of Brooke Shields, Tatum O'Neal, Katharine Hepburn and English rock star Adam Ant, but confesses to a gnawing loneliness that he seems unable to comprehend, much less come to grips with. Michael is often asked in interviews why he hasn't left home yet. His answer never varies. As he told the *Los Angeles Times* in 1981, "I think I'd die on my own. I'd be so lonely. Even at home, I'm lonely. I sit in my room sometimes and cry. It's so hard to make friends and there are some things you can't talk to your parents or family about. I sometimes walk around the neighborhood at night, just hoping to find someone to talk to. But I just end up coming home."

The image of one of popular music's reigning idols, a man who could have any woman he wanted with just a bend of his finger, walking around Encino in the dead of night looking for someone to talk to is a sad

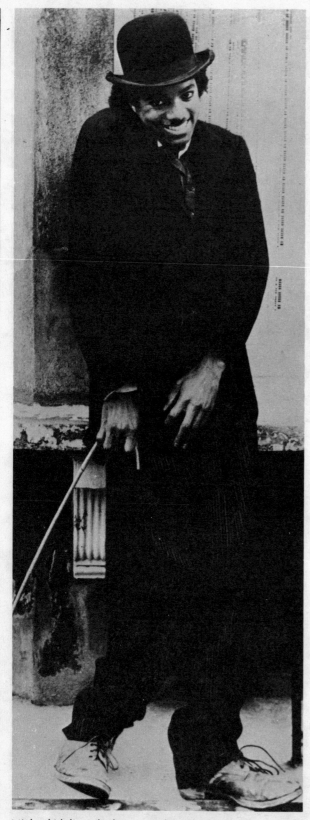
Michael idolizes the late comedian Charlie Chaplin.

one. Marriage would seem to be the logical answer but again, the spectre of the bubble intrudes. Michael's problem is to find a bride who, as the cliche goes, loves him for himself—not his name.

Although he has been romantically linked with both Tatum O'Neal and Brooke Shields, Michael demurs when asked about them. Actually, Michael allows as to how there *is* someone he loves and would marry in a moment. The lucky lady's name is Diana. As in Ross. When Michael dropped that information on a reporter from *Ebony*, the writer, perhaps feeling fantasy and reality bumping together on him, pushed ahead warily. Platonically, right? Michael was saying he loved his mentor platonically. Nope, replied Michael. Not platonically at all. He wants to marry her.

"He spends a lot of time, too much time, by himself," says Diana Ross of her would-be husband. "I try to get him out. I rented a boat and took my children and Michael on a cruise. Michael has a lot of people around him, but he's very afraid. I don't know why. I think it came from the early days."

Many people, who have had trouble making sense of the two distinct personalities (onstage and offstage) that inhabit Michael Jackson have speculated that he is gay. In fact, some magazines in the middle '70s ran lurid headlines spotlighting a supposed sex-change and/or marriage to actor Clifton Davis. The rumors exist primarily as catch-all explanations for complicated mysteries.

As Michael said in 1977 at the height of the rumor rampage, "People make up those things because they have nothing better to do. Some people let rumors like that get to them and have nervous breakdowns and stuff like that, but if I let that kind of talk get to me, it would only show how cheap I was. *I* know it's not true, so it doesn't bother me. I'm sure we must have plenty of fans who are gay and that doesn't bother me in the slightest, but *I'm* not gay."

Whether he is or not, speculation on the subject is something Michael is very keenly

A stunning performer, Michael is a perfectionist and spends hours practicing his craft. He says every Sunday, he fasts and dances—almost all day long!

79

aware of. At one time, Michael was considering an offer to star in a film version of *A Chorus Line* as a gay dancer. His major concern was, if he took the role, wouldn't that just help add new fire to the rumors? In the end, however, the question became academic. Producer Allan Carr nixed the idea, which he saw as a bad joke. "It's the worst idea I ever heard of," he complained. "It was ludicrous. Stunt casting."

Michael did get his shot at acting, however, in 1978's extravaganza, *The Wiz*. Predictably,

Mike's performing debut was a film wherein fantasy and reality bumped. He spent six months in New York during the filming, enduring daily the hours of makeup work that transformed him into the film's scarecrow. He has described the film as one of the most magical experiences of his life and critics, who were anything but kind to the film as a whole, seemed to agree that he was one of the few things that made it worthwhile.

As the scarecrow to Diana Ross' Dorothy,

Michael was a loose and funky soul, tripping his way down the yellow brick road in a purposely clumsy dance that modified only slightly the dazzling style for which he's become known. Of course, it was no surprise to moviegoers that Michael could dance. That was a given. What was a revelation, however, was the fact that Michael could act; drawing on his fabled wellspring of innocence and fantasy, Michael created a scarecrow to charm and beguile children and adults alike. His scarecrow was a figure both comic and sad as he joined the quest in search of a brain.

It was projects like *The Wiz* which led to a resurgence of talk that Michael would soon exit the Jacksons. That speculation was alive everywhere from the corporate suites of his record company to the rumor-heavy streets of Hollywood. But, as some observers noted, such talk is nothing new. They started even before Michael recorded *Got To Be There* at age 13; that album, his solo debut, was a smash. The rumors continued when Motown released "Ben," Michael's infamous and famous ode to a cinema rat.

At one point, the rumors got to be so

pervasive that Motown was moved to issue a statement that was almost peevish in tone. "We have emphatically stated in numerous press releases that the Jackson 5 will not split up. Michael's solo album is merely an extension of the fabulous creativity that exists in the group. They are multi-talented youngsters and there may well be other solo recordings by each of the others, vocal as well as instrumental. The idea that Michael is leaving is the figment of some fan magazine writer's overworked imagination."

Sure enough, when Michael's precedent-shattering *Off The Wall* album came out in 1978, the rumors surfaced again, but this time there was a twist to them. Many fans and observers began talking as if Michael had already left the group; the album sold over five million copies in the United States alone and Jackson became the first solo recording artist in history to place four singles from the same album in the Top 10; many people just couldn't see Michael staying with the group now that he had such a huge hit under his belt. Thus, some people began referring to the whole group as Michael Jackson—i.e., "Michael Jackson is giving a concert this weekend" or "Michael Jackson was on television last week." The fact is, even at the height of the 1978-79 Michaelmania, he made relatively few appearances without his brothers. The concerts and appearances that were being referred to as "Michael Jackson" shows were actually "Jackson" shows but for some people, it was almost as if the other brothers had ceased to exist.

Michael expressed concern that his brothers weren't getting their fair share of attention, but his concern didn't do much to stem the tide. His 1982 followup, *Thriller*, only helped to reignite the furor. Asked point-blank if he is contemplating an exit from the Jacksons, Michael is evasive. He told *Ebony* "Yes and no." He has told others that he tries to be guided by God and to do things when the time is right. At the time, he would say, the time isn't right. He would go on to add

that the time might be right in a week—or never. All of which sounds like a fancy way of saying that he hasn't decided—or perhaps doesn't want to leave. But it doesn't take genius-level perception to realize that the pressure he faces to make the move is monstrous.

It is, however, worth noting Michael's response to a plea from fans who wanted to see the Jacksons stay together because "you need your brothers and your brothers need you." As quoted in *Ebony*, he said, "I think fans would be concerned . . . and to see the split like that would break their hearts. Especially when groups start changing members . . . they lose originality and I'd really hate that. . . .

I let nature take its course. I let be what must be and if that is to come it's going to happen, because there are so many things I do want to do, really. I want to explore, experiment and branch out to do different things and it is always a time problem." In other words, yes and no. Sparrow-like shoulders weren't made to hoist mountain-like pressures.

Perhaps that's why Michael spent a great deal of the Jacksons' 1981 tour complaining about the rigors of the road—rigors he has, after all, endured since he was about 5—and announcing his retirement from performing. He appeared to recant that announcement not long after the tour ended, announcing a new tour that would reunite Jermaine with the group.

Getting away from hotels, returning to the safety of the bubble, may have had a lot to do with Michael's decision to reconsider. As he has said many times, he loves the stage, loves being loose and free in front of thousands of cheering fans, loves the opportunity performing gives him to get "out" of himself.

That love of the lights was probably born in Michael Joe Jackson right from the moment he first stood up in his kindergarten class to warble "Climb Every Mountain." From such humble origins, he exploded and became a

Right: Michael's association with producer Quincy Jones has proven to be the most profitable merger in music history. As a solo artist and lead singer of the Jacksons, Michael has broken records, both as a pop and R&B artist.

musical giant. He sings like an angel and dances like a demon. He is attracted . . . fascinated . . . by the guilelessness of children and animals, perhaps the only creatures in his sheltered world who will give him their unreserved love without asking something— an autograph, a performance, some money—in return. Not incidentially he is, at the bottom line, a good person. And that, too, you can blame on the boogie.

Their Musical Destiny

THE MUSIC

By rights, no young group should have progressed as far or grown as much. After all, the young groups—the so-called "bubblegum acts"—were primarily novelty attractions. From the Partridge Family to the Bay City Rollers, such acts specialized in image over substance, gimmickry over real talent. They offered kids heroes—heroes their own age who looked and sounded the same and shared similar interests and concerns. For the old folks, youth groups offered welcome assurance that at least *some* kids were still clean-cut and presentable.

But no one expected longevity from the kid groups. As voices changed and chubby faces became creased with the cares of adulthood, most such acts did a fade-out you could set your watch by. That the Jacksons didn't pull such a fade is reflective of a number of factors: "Motown's" careful planning, the group's own luck and, not the least of the equation, talent. With several of the brothers now past the magic age of 30 and the group well into its second decade of hit-making, it's safe to say that the quick fade is something the Jacksons don't really have to worry about now.

One does not sell 100 million-plus records without doing something right. There have been flops, of course—notably, Jackie's solo album, which the group reportedly jokes sold perhaps three copies. But the brothers have hit more often than they have missed and theirs is one of popular music's tightest, most invigorating bodies of work. It includes:

"I Want You Back."

"ABC."

"The Love You Save,"— although "ABC" and "The Love You Save" weren't in the same league with "I Want You Back" (few songs are), they were nonetheless amiably energetic outings that built upon the "bubblegum soul" standard set by the first hit.

"I Found That Girl"— Jermaine leads the group through a happy ballad that captures eloquently the rapture of a young man in first love. "Mama," sings Jermaine, "life for me now is a

87

new sensation/Just like you said it would be/With the right situation/Now love has a meaning/And I have a goal/This feeling inside me now/Makes Yester-me a hundred years old." It's worth noting here that although the Jackson 5's early music was roundly criticized in some corners for its lack of substance and maturity, such criticism has been shown to be woefully short-sighted. Lightweight though the uptempo tunes may have been in terms of lyrics, the brothers whisked through them with a professionalism beyond their years. And on a ballad like this one, the brothers bring a timeless sense of . . . rightness . . . to lyrics any lovestruck young man can surely relate to.

"I'll Be There"— This is, far and away, the best

of the Jackson 5 ballads, a shimmering, gossamer love song blessed with a convincing lead from Michael and a nice harmony arrangement. A song like this is a prime example of why it was often easy to forget the fact that the Jackson 5 were just little boys.

"Never Can Say Goodbye"— Actor Clifton Davis ("That's My Mama") composed this song, which has since been covered by a number of people, including disco diva Gloria Gaynor. The J-5 version was billowy and elusive, anchored only by Michael's straight-ahead, no-nonsense delivery at the core.

"Goin' Back To Indiana"— The Jackson 5 varied the "bubblegum soul" formula quite a bit

Among the group's many awards has been honors from the NAACP, the organization which sponsors the Image Awards.

on this tune and it's one of the most interesting of the early upbeat numbers. It's a chunky rock 'n' roll number, brought to life by a chugging rhythm section, some mildly scorching lead guitar from Tito, and a loose, spry performance from you-know-who.

"Lookin' Through The Window"— This song was very transitory in feel, as though the producers had the idea it was time to change the group's sound, but no firm idea of where to take them. Thus, rather than being a bold step in a new direction, "Window," though pleasant enough, is curiously laid back and directionless. It's middle of the road.

"Skywriter" and **"Hallelujah Day"**— Both these tunes harken back to the earlier bubblegum soul sound, but at this stage in the group's development, that sound fit them rather awkwardly. There's energy a plenty in both numbers, but one cannot long escape the feeling that the five were merely going through the motions here.

"Get It Together"— A swift, funky one, that slices open in high gear and doesn't waver. This tune updated the Jackson 5 tremendously; when it was first released, many people found it hard to believe this was the same group of "ABC" fame.

"Dancin' Machine"— This tune was a worldwide bestseller, and for good reason. It rides with the smooth assuredness of a perfectly engineered vehicle. Michael has fun with the tricky lead lines

89

while his brothers contribute spurts of bright harmony behind him. The song was always a treat to watch in performance; when the instrumental break comes and the band locks into a "machine-like" groove, Michael and his brothers do some lock-step robot dancing that has to be seen to be appreciated.

"I Am Love"— "Love" was one of the most adventurous Jackson 5 songs. It begins slowly and reflectively with an electric keyboard mirroring Jermaine's coolly-impassioned vocals. Subtly, almost imperceptibly, that slow tempo builds to a tense dramatic instrumental break, Michael takes over, and cool vocals go out the window in favor of a fired-up beat, accented sharply by drums and echoing electric guitar.

"Forever Came Today"— It's hard to improve upon Rolling Stones' review of this updated Supremes oldie. Vince Aletti wrote, "(Producer Brian Holland) takes what was once a slight, forgettable song, given a measured dramatic reading by Diana Ross, and explodes it. Chunks of music shoot off like fireworks, chanted choruses carom from speaker to speaker and Michael sings with inspired abandon. The song builds and breaks several times, each time intensifying its effect until the final choruses are red hot."

"Enjoy Yourself"— "Enjoy" isn't particularly the deepest or most meaningful song one is ever likely to stumble across. What it does have going for it, however, is a simple infectiousness that's hard to resist. Its perky, jangling rhythm structure invites singalong and makes "Enjoy" one of those rare songs that stays with you long after the record ends.

"Blame It To The Boogie"— The Jacksons essentially reprised earlier triumphs when they crafted "Boogie." The song moves with the unpredicable bounce of a superball, bounding out of the speakers with a sound that seems irresistibly simple and bubblegummish on the surface. It's only when you get into the tune, survey its vocal arrangement and the aching *adult* urgency of its lyrics that you realize the resemblance to past tunes is only superficial.

Loyal London fans wait outside the Churchill Hotel for a glimpse of the Jacksons. Such crowds are a familiar sight to the family, although they often feel uneasy to be surrounded by masses who hail them as idols.

"Shake Your Body (Down To The Ground)"

— "Shake" was the first hit to feature the "new" Jacksons' sound. The fact that that sound has since become one of the most imitated in music serves as indication that the guys were on to something big. "Shake" is bare bones boogie; it's music stripped of gimmickry and instrumental pretension. All that's left is the single most important element—drive. And, powered by bass, keyboards and a little synthesizer frill, "Shake" is exactly that—driven. It offers clean, uncluttered lines of dance music that are broken only

90

briefly and unobstrusively for a little horn fill here and there.

It's fitting that "Shake" was such a big hit, coming even as it did at the overproduced height of the disco phenomenon. It offered the same thing disco did—an unbeatable beat—but without disco's tendency to overstate, productionwise.

"Lovely One"—This song was an obvious attempt to duplicate the success of "Shake"—same stripped down lines of music, same relentless rhythm. Lyrically, it's a better constructed tune (after all, "Shake" was really all chorus: "Let's dance/Let's shout/Shake your body down to the ground"), but that doesn't make it a better tune outright. It still comes off as an entertaining sequel to the main event.

Michael's Solos

"Ben"—The fact that this tune, from a movie soundtrack of the same name, is an ode to a rat sort of takes away from any empathy its sensitive lyrics might create. Meaning that the song is a soaring, soul-searching performance until one gets right down to the nitty gritty fact that Michael isn't singing about a human friend here, but a rodent. Still, the song is a perennial favorite of Jackson fans.

"Got To Be There"— I'll Be There"—by the Jackson 5 is far and away the better song, but "Got To Be There" shares many of the same elements: restrained, gossamer instrumentation and an impassioned lead vocal. Interestingly, singer Chaka Khan got hold of the song in 1982 and threw out its polite delicacy in favor of a soaring unleashed sensuality. Many feel that hers was the better version of the song.

"Rockin' Robin"—A chipper, cheerful and rather inconsequential updating of a golden oldie.

"I Wanna Be Where You Are"—When he was in his middle-teens, nobody could lay a glove on Michael Jackson when it came to handling a bright, sunshiny pop melody. Occasionally, his facility with that sort of music opened Mike up to charges that he was a lightweight. This tune is probably the sort of song the critics were thinking of when they leveled those blasts, but "I Wanna Be Where You Are" is certainly spry and listenable even if it's not the most complex piece that ever came down the pike.

"Don't Stop Till You Get Enough"—The landmark *Off The Wall* album has already won its place as one of recent history's best-selling projects, thanks largely to a handful of monster hit singles like this. Michael blasts it open with a squeal that seems to signify now is the time for a release of pent-up fury. "Don't Stop" it's a cool kinetic beat that finds Michael in the saddle near the top of his tenor, threatening to explode, but never quite surrendering control.

"Rock With You"—This tune moves along at a lazy pace for a dance number, seemingly uncaring of the old axiom that you've got to work up a sweat if you want 'em to dance. "Rock" doesn't work up a sweat, doesn't even come close, as a matter of fact. The tune glides through, enigmatic as a black limousine and therefore, just as

captivating. Its appeal as a dance track is hard to pin down, but undeniable nonetheless. "Rock" offers a midtempo saunter across the dance floor —and it works.

"Working Day And Night"—This song is the other side of "Rock With You." Where that song is a laid back tune, "Working Day And Night" is electric. Frentic. It's filled with a nervous, itchy energy that never quite dissipates itself as the rhythm builds to sharp break after break. Michael sings in a furtive whisper, as though he's eager to confide his frustrations and passions but doesn't like being caught in such a compromised position.

"She's Out Of My Life"—It is said that although producer Quincy Jones did take after take of this song, Michael was unable to get through it even once without sobbing. With anyone else, that might sound terribly corny. With Michael, it just sounds terribly . . . Michael. Indeed, if you listen to the studio version of this tune or to the live version, you can hear his voice trembling and the sound of quiet crying. And no wonder. "She's Out Of My Life" is a stark, anguished, bitter ballad of naked recrimination. Jones was careful to understate his production here, leaving Michael plenty of room to move around in. Michael responds by wringing every last tear and nuance from the lyrics. "She's Out Of My Life" is a terribly affecting number.

"Thriller"—This number is a typical Quincy Jones production, gaudy with flash and gimmickry. Doors creak and slam, wind howls, Vincent Price (of all people) raps—and it works. "Thriller" is good fun, spooky in an amiable sort of way.

"Beat It"—Michael turned to rock 'n' roll for a moment on this tune, and the result is a blistering rhythm for dance floor fanatics. But, beyond that, the song's lyrics paint a despairing picture of stardom and adulation as an attractive, yet deadly cage. Do we have a self-portrait here?

"Billie Jean"—As one critic put it, Michael sings this song as if his very life depended upon it. It's

Over the years the group has done many benefits especially those which involve children.

The Jackson women: (Clockwise) Enid (Jackie's wife), Julie (Randy's former girlfriend), Hazel Gordy (Jermaine's wife whose father Berry is a Chairman of the Board of Motown Records), Dee Dee (Tito's wife) and Carol (Marlon's spouse).

one/But the kid is *not* my son." But the song leads us to wonder who is really the deceiver here as Michael appears to struggle with conflicting passions and unclear emotions, even going so far as to admit that "the kid" has eyes that "look just like mine." Hmmmm.

Jermaine's Solos

"Daddy's Home"— Jermaine, he of the cool, easy-going vocals, really shines in this updated oldie. The background vocal arrangement is likewise a gem, with the singers do-wopping and rat-a-tatling in imitation of drums "Daddy's Home" is gorgeously and unapologetically romantic.

"Let's Be Young Tonight"— This number tries to muster up some energy and Jermaine is working hard, but it's really no dice. The tune is nice enough, but ultimately quite forgettable.

"My Touch Of Madness"— "Madness" sort of oozes in at you surrealistically, anchored to earth only by Jermaine at the center of a sexy, romantic lead vocal. For some reason, the song was not a big success with either critics or fans.

"Let's Get Serious"— Stevie Wonder stepped in to produce this number, and gave Jermaine a monster. It has a ferocious beat that manhandles a casual listener, wrestling him or her into submission. The song is all muscle; it has such a strong rhythm that Jermaine could easily become superfluous—just another production decoration. But he rides the tune well, showing off some growling, snapping lead vocals borrowed from Stevie Wonder. "Serious," not surprisingly, was the first big hit of Jermaine's post-Jackson solo career.

"Let Me Tickle Your Fancy"— Members of the rock group Devo guest starred on this new wave-inspired bit of whimsy. It proved a different direction for Jermaine who, by 1982, was showing signs of becoming mired once again in the directionless daze from which "Serious" had seemingly freed him.

a tale of a paternity suit slapped on Mike by an evil witch named Billie Jean. As the song slides along on it deceptively unhurried way, Michael counterpoints with desperate lead vocals as if he's just *got* to convince someone that Billie Jean is doing him in. He sings, "Billie Jean is *not* my lover/She's just a girl who claims that I am the

"When we were tiny little boys /
We used to dance, we used to
sing / Before we even learned to
crawl or walk / As we grew up,
we didn't change / I guess we
knew right from the start / We
loved the spotlight and the stage
/ 'Cause we were born to
entertain."

—the Jackson 5, from
"We're Here to Entertain You"